The Further
Adventures of Toad

from
The Wind in the Willows

Written by
KENNETH GRAHAME

Abridged and illustrated by
INGA MOORE

TED SMART

The Further Adventures of Toad

The door of the hollow tree faced eastwards, so Toad was called at an early hour. Sitting up, he rubbed his eyes, looking round for familiar stone wall and barred window; then, with a leap of the heart, remembered everything – his escape, his flight, his pursuit; best of all, that he was free!

Free! He marched forth into the morning sun. He had the world to himself, that early summer morning. The dewy woodland was solitary and still; the green fields were his own to do as he liked with; the road, when he reached it, in that loneliness that was everywhere, seemed to be looking for company. Toad, however, was looking for something that could tell him clearly which way he ought to go.

The road was presently joined by a little canal. Round a bend in the canal came plodding a solitary horse, stooping forward as if in anxious thought. From his collar stretched a long line, taut, but dipping with his stride, the further part of it dripping pearly drops. Toad let the horse pass, and stood waiting for what the fates were sending him.

With a swirl of water, the barge slid up alongside of him, its occupant a big stout woman wearing a linen sun-bonnet.

"A nice morning, ma'am!" she remarked to Toad.

"I dare say it *is*, ma'am!" responded Toad, "to them that's not in trouble, like what I am. My married daughter, she sends for me to come at once; so off I comes, fearing the worst, as you will understand, ma'am, if you're a mother too. And I've left my washing business to look after itself, and my young children, ma'am; and I've lost all my money, and my way."

"Where might your married daughter be living, ma'am?" asked the barge-woman.

"Near Toad Hall, ma'am," replied Toad.

"Toad Hall? I'm going that way," replied the barge-woman. "Come along in the barge with me, and I'll give you a lift."

She steered the barge close to the bank, and Toad stepped lightly on board.

"So you're in the washing business?" said the barge-woman. "And are you *very* fond of washing?"

"I love it," said Toad. "I simply dote on it. Never so happy as when I've got both arms in the wash-tub."

"What a bit of luck," observed the barge-woman.

"Why, what do you mean?" asked Toad nervously.

"Well, there's a heap of things of mine that you'll find in a corner of the cabin. If you'll just put them through the wash-tub as we go along, it'll be a real help to me."

"I might not do 'em as you like," said Toad. "I'm more used to gentlemen's things myself. It's my special line."

"You do the washing you are so fond of," replied the barge-woman. "Don't deprive me of the pleasure of giving you a treat!"

Toad was fairly cornered. He looked for escape, saw he was too far from the bank for a flying leap, and resigned himself to his fate. "If it comes to that," he thought in desperation, "I suppose any fool can *wash*!"

He fetched tub, soap, and other necessaries from the cabin, selected a few garments, and set to.

A half-hour passed, and every minute of it saw Toad getting crosser and crosser. Nothing he could do to the things seemed to do them good. He tried coaxing, slapping, punching. His back ached and he noticed with dismay that his paws were beginning to get all crinkly. Now Toad was very proud of his paws. He muttered under his breath words that should never pass the lips of washerwomen or Toads; and lost the soap, for the fiftieth time.

The barge-woman laughed till tears ran down her cheeks.

"Pretty washerwoman you are!" she gasped. "Never washed so much as a dish-clout in your life, I'll lay!"

Toad's temper, which had been simmering for some time, now boiled over.

"You common, low, *fat* barge-woman!" he shouted; "don't you dare to talk to your betters like that! Washerwoman indeed! I would have you know that I am a Toad, a very well-known, respected, distinguished Toad! I may be under a bit of a cloud at present, but I will *not* be laughed at by a barge-woman!"

The woman peered under his bonnet. "Why, so you are!" she cried. "Well, I never! a horrid, nasty, crawly Toad! And in my nice clean barge, too! That is a thing that I will *not* have."

One big mottled arm shot out and caught Toad by a fore-leg. Then the world turned upside down, the barge seemed to flit across the sky, and Toad found himself flying through the air.

The water, when he reached it, proved cold, though not enough to quell his spirit. He rose to the surface, and when he had wiped the duckweed out of his eyes the first thing he saw was the barge-woman looking back at him over the stern of the barge and laughing.

He struck out for the shore, touched land, and climbed up the steep bank. Then, gathering his wet skirts well over his arms, he started to run after the barge, as fast as his legs would carry him, wild for revenge.

The barge-woman was still laughing when he drew up level with her. "Put yourself through your mangle, washerwoman," she called out, "and iron your face and crimp it, and you'll pass for quite a decent-looking Toad!"

Toad never paused to reply. Revenge was what he wanted, not cheap, windy, verbal triumphs, though he had a thing or two he would have liked to say. Running swiftly on he overtook the horse, unfastened the tow-rope, jumped on the horse's back, and urged it to a gallop by kicking it vigorously in the sides. He steered for the open country, abandoning the tow-path, and swinging his steed down a rutty lane. "Stop, stop, stop!" shouted the barge-woman.

"I've heard that song before," said Toad, laughing,

as he continued to spur his steed onward.

The barge-horse was not capable of any sustained effort, and its gallop soon subsided into a trot, and its trot to an easy walk; but Toad was quite contented with this. He had recovered his temper, now he had done something he thought really clever; and he was satisfied to jog along quietly in the sun, trying to forget how very long it was since he had had a square meal.

He had travelled some miles, his horse and he, and he was feeling drowsy in the hot sunshine, when the horse stopped, lowered his head, and began to nibble the grass; and Toad just saved himself from falling off.

He looked about him and found he was on a wide common,
dotted with patches of gorse and bramble as far as he could see.
Near him stood a dingy gipsy caravan, and a man was sitting,
very busy smoking and staring into the wide world.
A fire of sticks was burning near by, and over the fire
hung an iron pot, and out of that pot came forth
smells – warm, rich, and varied smells.
Toad sniffed, and looked at
the gipsy; and the
gipsy smoked,
and looked
at him.

Presently the gipsy remarked in a careless way, "Want to sell that there horse of yours?"

It had not occurred to Toad to turn the horse into cash.

"O no," he said, "I'm too fond of him, and he dotes on me. All the same, how much might you be disposed to offer me?"

The gipsy looked the horse over, and he looked Toad over with equal care. "Shillin' a leg," he said briefly.

"A shilling a leg?" cried Toad. "I must work that out."

He climbed down off his horse and did sums on his fingers. At last he said, "That comes to four shillings. O no; I could not think of accepting four shillings for this young horse of mine."

"Well," said the gipsy, "I'll make it five shillings, and that's three-and-sixpence more than the animal's worth."

Toad pondered. He was hungry and penniless, and still some way from home, and enemies might be looking for him. To one in such a situation, five shillings may very well appear a large sum of money. On the other hand, it did not seem very much to get for a horse. But then, the horse hadn't cost him anything. At last he said firmly, "You hand me six shillings and sixpence, and as much breakfast as I can eat out of that iron pot of yours. In return, I will make over to you my spirited young horse, with all the harness and trappings on him, freely thrown in. If that's not good enough, say so, and I'll be getting on. I know a man near here who's wanted this horse for years."

The gipsy grumbled frightfully, and declared he'd be ruined. But in the end he lugged a dirty canvas bag out of the depths of his trouser-pocket, and counted out six shillings and six-pence into Toad's paw. Then he disappeared into the caravan, and returned with a large iron plate. He tilted the pot, and a stream of hot rich stew gurgled into it. Toad took the plate on his lap, and stuffed, and stuffed, and stuffed, and kept asking for more, and the gipsy never grudged it him. He thought he had never eaten so good a breakfast in all his life.

When Toad had taken as much stew on board as he thought he could possibly hold, he got up and took an affectionate farewell of the horse; and the gipsy, who knew the riverside well, gave him directions which way to go, and he set forth on his travels again in the best possible spirits. The sun was shining brightly, his wet clothes were quite dry, he had money in his pockets once more, and he had had a substantial meal, hot and nourishing, and felt big, and strong, and self-confident.

As he tramped along gaily, he thought of his adventures and escapes, and how when things seemed at their worst he had always managed to find a way out; and his pride and conceit began to swell within him. He got so puffed up that he made up a song in praise of himself, and sang it at the top of his voice. It was perhaps the most conceited song that any animal ever composed:

> *The world has held great Heroes,*
> *As history-books have showed;*
> *But never a name to go down to fame*
> *Compared with that of Toad!*
>
> *The clever men at Oxford*
> *Know all that there is to be knowed.*
> *But they none of them know one half as much*
> *As intelligent Mr Toad!*
>
> *The Queen and her Ladies-in-waiting*
> *Sat at the window and sewed.*
> *She cried, "Look! who's that handsome man?"*
> *They answered, "Mr Toad."*

There was a great deal more, but too dreadfully conceited to be written down. These are some of the milder verses.

He sang as he walked, and walked as he sang. But his pride was shortly to have a severe fall.

After some miles he reached the high road, and as he turned into it and glanced along its white length, he saw approaching him a speck that turned into a dot and then a blob, and then into something very familiar; and a "poop, poop!" fell on his delighted ear.

"This is something like!" said the excited Toad. "This is real life again, this is the world from which I have been missed so long! I will hail them, my brothers of the wheel, and they will give me a lift, and, with luck, it may even end in my driving up to Toad Hall! That will be one in the eye for Badger!"

He stepped out into the road to hail the motor-car, which came along at an easy pace, when suddenly he became very pale, his knees shook, and he doubled up with a sickening pain in his interior. And well he might, for the approaching car was the very one he had stolen out of the yard of the Red Lion Hotel! And the people in it were the very same people he had sat and watched at luncheon in the coffee-room!

He sank down in a heap, murmuring, "It's all up! Prison again! Dry bread and water!" The motor-car drew nearer till at last he heard it stop. Two gentlemen got out and one of them said, "O dear! this is very sad! A poor washerwoman has fainted in the road! Perhaps she is overcome by the heat, poor creature. Let us lift her into the car and take her to the nearest village, where doubtless she has friends."

They tenderly lifted Toad into the motor-car and propped him up with soft cushions, and proceeded on their way.

When Toad knew that he was not recognized, his courage began to revive, and he opened first one eye, then the other.

"Look!" said one of the gentlemen, "she is better already. The fresh air is doing her good. How do you feel now, ma'am?"

"Thank you kindly, sir," said Toad in a feeble voice, "I'm feeling a great deal better! I was thinking, if I might sit on the front seat there, beside the driver, where I could get the fresh air full in my face, I should soon be all right again."

"What a sensible woman!" said the gentleman. "Of course you shall." So they helped Toad into the front seat beside the driver, and on they went once more.

Toad was almost himself again by now. And he turned to the driver at his side. "Please, sir," he said, "I wish you would let me try and drive a little, it looks so easy and I should like to be able to tell my friends that once I had driven a motor-car!"

The driver laughed so heartily that the gentleman inquired what the matter was. When he heard he said, "Bravo, ma'am! I like your spirit. Let her have a try."

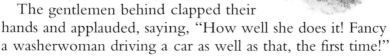

Toad scrambled into the driver's seat, took the steering-wheel in his hands, listened to the instructions given him, and set the car in motion, very slowly and carefully.

The gentlemen behind clapped their hands and applauded, saying, "How well she does it! Fancy a washerwoman driving a car as well as that, the first time!"

Toad went a little faster; then faster still, and faster.

He heard the gentlemen call out, "Be careful, washerwoman!" And this annoyed him, and he began to lose his head.

The driver tried to interfere, but he pinned him down with one elbow, and put on full speed. "Washerwoman, indeed!" he shouted recklessly. "Ho, ho! I am the Toad, the motor-car snatcher, the prison-breaker, the Toad who always escapes!"

With a cry of horror the party flung themselves on him. "Seize him!" they cried. "Seize the Toad who stole our motor-car!"

Alas! they should have remembered to stop the motor-car before playing pranks of that sort. With a half-turn of the wheel Toad sent the car crashing through the low roadside hedge. One mighty bound, a violent shock, and the wheels of the car were churning up the thick mud of a horse-pond.

Toad found himself flying through the air with the delicate curve of a swallow. He liked the motion, and was just beginning to wonder whether he would develop wings when he landed with a thump, in the soft rich grass of a meadow. Sitting up, he could just see the car in the pond; the gentlemen and driver were floundering helplessly in the water. He picked himself up and set off running across country as hard as he could, till he was breathless and weary, and had to settle into an easy walk. When he had recovered his breath and was able to think calmly, he began to laugh, and he laughed till he had to sit down under a hedge. "Ho, ho!" he cried. "Toad, as usual comes out on top! Who got them to give him a lift? Who persuaded them into letting him drive? Who landed them all in a horse-pond? Who escaped, flying gaily through the air, leaving them in the mud? Why, Toad, of course; clever Toad, great Toad, *good* Toad! How clever I am! How clever, how very clev—"

A slight noise behind him made him turn his head and look. O horror!

About two fields off, a chauffeur in his leather gaiters and two large rural policemen were running towards him as hard as they could go!

Toad pelted away again. "O my!" he gasped. "O my! O my!"

He glanced back, and saw to his dismay that they were gaining on him. On he ran. He did his best, but he was a fat animal, and his legs were short, and still they gained. He could hear them close behind him now. He struggled on wildly, looking back over his shoulder at the enemy, when suddenly the earth failed under his feet, he grasped at the air, and —

splash! he found himself head over ears in deep, rapid water;

in his panic he had run straight into the river!

He rose to the surface and tried to grasp the reeds and rushes that grew along the water's edge, but the stream was so strong it tore them out of his hands. "O my!" gasped Toad, "if ever I steal a motor-car again!" – then down he went, and came up breathless and spluttering. Presently he saw a big dark hole in the bank, just above his head, and as the stream bore him past, he reached up and caught hold of the edge and held on. Slowly and with difficulty he drew himself up out of the water. There he remained for some minutes, puffing and panting.

As he stared before him into the dark hole, some bright small thing shone and twinkled in its depths, moving towards him.

A face grew up around it, a familiar face!

Brown and small, with whiskers.

Grave and round, with neat ears and silky hair.

It was the Water Rat!